When I Grow Up, I Want To Be Myself

When I Grow Up, I Want To Be Myself

Written by A. Cole
Illustrated by Lea Embeli

This book is dedicated to
the two loves of my life,
Dezmond Seifu and our beautiful
baby girl, Aria.

Many people are going to try to tell you who and what to be. The only one who can make those decisions for you, is yourself.

-A. Cole

Written by Ashley Chambliss
Illustrations by Lea Embeli
Edited by Tabbye Chavous-Sellers Ph.D

I'm a little different, the things I say and do.

I feel like I can be anything, or anyone I choose.

I believe I make the best choices for myself!

I know I can pick my favorite things from my shelf.

One morning, I said flowers and boots, beads, and bows,

I was unique and original from my head to my toes.

I headed to school and expected no surprises.

I walked into a room of <u>colorless</u> shirts of all sizes.

No one dressed like me. I wondered WHY?

Was I uncool? Was I different? All of a sudden, I felt real shy.

To make matters worse, that day was career day,

Everyone had props with them and a speech to say.

It seemed just about everyone knew what they wanted to be...

And I felt sad, because it was everyone but ME.

I thought about all the things I thought I could do.

A teacher?

A lawyer? I had to choose!

Lucas stood up and said, “I want to be an astronaut!”

Renee said, “I want to be a doctor!”

Ira said, “I want to be an engineer and design bridges!”

And I thought to myself, what to be...what to be...

All the jobs I heard were nice, but those are not for me.

That night, I drifted off to sleep,

It was so quiet, the dogs made no peep.

I dreamt about who I wanted to be.

When I closed my eyes I was able to see...

I am kind, I am giving, I am unique and crazy!

When I grow up, I don't know who I want to be.
All I know is that I will be ME.

I want to be MYSELF today and forever!

The next day before school, I dressed myself with pride,

and raised my hand to share with no props at my side.

I told them that we should love what makes us one of a kind,

Not knowing what response I'd find.

All the smiles I got that day made me as happy as can be

I got high fives for standing up and just being me!

So, the moral of this story is: stop listening
to what other people may say.
It's okay to be different,
and try things your own way.
(and please don't decide what you want to
be today)
Instead, think about what type
of person you want to be
when you grow up,
someone kind, and loving your mom & dad
would love to raise up!

Be the best you, YOU can be.

The End.